SEAN TAYLOR is a children's writer, storyteller and teacher.
His books for Frances Lincoln include the Purple Class series, *The Great Snake*,
Who Ate Auntie Iris?, *The Grizzly Bear with the Frizzly Hair*
and *Crocodiles are the Best Animals of All*, which,
along with *Purple Class and the Half-Eaten Sweater*,
was shortlisted for the Roald Dahl Prize 2009.
Sean lives partly in England and partly in Brazil.
www.seantaylorstories.com

HANNAH SHAW has written and illustrated many critically acclaimed
picture books. These include *Crocodiles are the Best Animals of All*,
The Grizzly Bear with the Frizzly Hair and *Who Ate Auntie Iris?* with Sean Taylor,
and *Evil Weasel*, *Erroll* and *School for Bandits*, which she wrote and illustrated.
Hannah lives in Gloucestershire. For details of her workshops
for schools and libraries, visit her website.
www.hannahshawillustrator.co.uk

D1328849

For Constantin - ST
For Ellen - HS

JANETTA OTTER-BARRY BOOKS

Q Quarto Knows

Text copyright © Sean Taylor 2013
Illustrations copyright © Hannah Shaw 2013

First published in Great Britain in 2013 and in the USA in 2014 by
Frances Lincoln Children's Books,
74-77 White Lion Street, London N1 9PF
www.franceslincoln.com

First paperback published in Great Britain in 2014

A catalogue record for this book is available from the British Library.

ISBN 978-1-84780-983-4
Illustrated with pen and ink and scanned textures

Set in Clearface Gothic LT

Printed in China

1 3 5 7 9 8 6 4 2

WE HAVE LIFT-OFF!

by **Sean Taylor**

Illustrated by
Hannah Shaw

Frances Lincoln
Children's Books

You're looking at the first chicken in outer space, **which was me.**

You see, I used to live on Mr Tanner's Farm. And it really was a RIGHT OLD DUMP.

Mr Tanner poisoned
the air with smoke. . .

and filled the
river with junk. . .

and cut down
all the trees. . .

and crammed us animals
into a crumbling barn.

But his house just kept getting BIGGER

and **BIGGER**

and **BIGGER!**

We animals couldn't take it any more.

So we held a meeting in a `top-secret` location,
to see if there was anything we could do.

And we decided to do
something...

We built an intergalactic rocket so that we could escape, away from Mr Tanner, and up to the CLEAR, CLEAN STARS.

It was a difficult plan. But if it worked, we were sure that news would spread. Then ANIMALS ALL ROUND THE WORLD would start doing THE SAME THING!

Because, let's face it, animals have had enough of trying to share our planet with *people*.

THE PLAN

* USE JUNK.

EARTH
PEOPLE = TOO MUCH JUNK.

* BUILD ROCKET

ANIMALS ESCAPE!

$$Z = \frac{xy^2 \times 200,00000}{\sqrt{50,00101}}$$

People just keep on
MESSING THINGS UP.

TO THE MOON...

The pig who designed our rocket reckoned it was strong enough to carry us all. But he said someone had go on a **TEST FLIGHT**.

And that was when I got chosen!

I was given moonboots, a space helmet and a map. And a supply of **cornflakes** that looked enough to last for a whole life.

I was shown the START button (which I was supposed to press at the start).

START

EMERGENCY
ABANDON
MISSION

And the EMERGENCY ABANDON MISSION button (which I wasn't supposed to press, except in an emergency).

Then,
5 - 4 - 3 - 2 - 1......
WE HAVE LIFT-OFF!

Up I went... away from the litter and clutter of Mr Tanner's farm!

First of all, everything went fine.

I was in radio contact
with the Flight Director at
ANIMAL MISSION CONTROL.
And I was ON MY WAY
TO THE STARS!

But there was a problem.

I was holding the map
upside-**down**.

And suddenly the rocket was heading
back towards our planet.

We had to do another TEST FLIGHT and this time a very clever rabbit was chosen.

He put on moonboots and a space helmet.

He was given a map and a big box of carrots.

Then,
5 - 4 - 3 - 2 - 1......
WE HAVE LIFT-OFF!

Up went the rabbit...
out of the smog and smoke
of Mr Tanner's farm!

First of all everything went fine.
The rabbit was ON HIS WAY
TO THE **STARS!**

Then there was a problem.

I think the rabbit got nervous.

He started eating carrots
very fast. . .

and the box got stuck over his head.
He bumped the steering wheel and the rocket started **heading back.**

"DON'T COME BACK!"
said the Flight Director.

But it was **too late.**
The rabbit couldn't get the box off, and the only way was

down.

We still had to do a successful
TEST FLIGHT, and a very calm
sheep was chosen next.

She was given moonboots,
a space helmet, a map and
a supply of cabbage leaves
in LITTLE boxes that she
couldn't get stuck
over her head.

DON'T PANIC!

Then,

5 - 4 - 3 - 2 - 1 .....
WE HAVE LIFT-OFF!

Up went the sheep...
away from the muck and
junk of Mr Tanner's farm!

First of all, everything went fine.
The sheep was ON HER WAY
TO THE STARS!

Then there was a problem.

The sheep fell asleep.
What's worse, she leant
her head on the
EMERGENCY
ABANDON MISSION
button so the rocket
turned automatically
back.

"For Goodness' sake!"
said the Flight Director.
"DON'T
COME
BACK!"

But it was **too late.**

The sheep was asleep, and the only way **was down.**

And that was when Mr Tanner came
to find out what the noise was about.

AND HE DISCOVERED
OUR ROCKET!

He seemed to think
it was funny... because
he laughed at it. Then he
just looked inside, as if
it was his.

But the joke was on him, because somehow
he pressed the START button.

Then,
5 - 4 - 3 - 2 - 1.....
WE HAVE LIFT-OFF!

It wasn't what we'd planned.
But actually it was better than
trying to escape in the rocket.

And news has spread.

Now ANIMALS ALL ROUND THE WORLD
are building intergalactic rockets and sending
people like Mr Tanner up to the stars.

So if you're one of the people who makes
a mess of our planet... **WATCH OUT!**

It could be **your** turn next!

MORE GREAT PICTURE BOOKS BY SEAN TAYLOR AND HANNAH SHAW

CROCODILES ARE THE BEST ANIMALS OF ALL
Sean Taylor
Illustrated by Hannah Shaw

Their ears may wiggle
And their teeth may be wonky,
But nothing is better than being a donkey.
Is it true? There's a crocodile who doesn't agree!

Shortlisted for the Roald Dahl Funny Prize 2009

"Picture book of the season." *Bookseller*

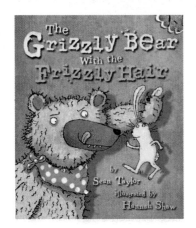

THE GRIZZLY BEAR WITH THE FRIZZLY HAIR
Sean Taylor
Illustrated by Hannah Shaw

There was nothing left to eat in the woods.
The Grizzly Bear with the Frizzly Hair had eaten it all.
And that's why he was looking bad-tempered and hungry.
That's why he was on the prowl....
So how do you think this itzy-bitzy rabbit felt
when they came face to face?

WHO ATE AUNTIE IRIS?
Sean Taylor
Illustrated by Hannah Shaw

Where Auntie Iris lives, there are bears on the first floor,
a crocodile on the second floor and wolves on the third floor.
When Auntie Iris goes missing, one brave little chinchilla
is determined to find out WHAT has happened to Auntie Iris...
A deliciously suspenseful mystery story for young children.

Frances Lincoln titles are available from all good bookshops.
You can also buy books and find out more about your favourite titles,
authors and illustrators on our website: www.franceslincoln.com